BIG BAD BILL
on the Naughty Step

written by **M**ark Sperring

il' **M**cLaughlin

PUFFIN

One day, Sam found himself sitting somewhere he didn't much care to sit.

It wasn't snuggled up on the sofa with Dad.

Or riding along
with Rover . . .

or watching a film with
his big sister Nellie.

Sam was sat somewhere not quite so nice or half as much fun . . .

Sam was sat on the naughty step.

The naughty step was right at the bottom of the stairs and only a hop, *skip* and **shiver me timbers** away from Pirate Cove.

So Sam was not one bit surprised to look up and see a certain someone standing there.

Slithering seaweed!
It was **Captain Buckleboots!**

"Have **you** been naughty **AGAIN**?" Sam asked.

Captain Buckleboots sat himself down with a sigh.
    "Sam, Sam, Sam," he said. "I've been **SO** naughty.
I called my shipmates scurvy scoundrels
and left them stranded . . .

just because they wanted to build sandcastles and eat
ice cream instead of helping me dig for treasure."

But before Sam could say, "How terrible!"
the front door *squeaked* open . . .

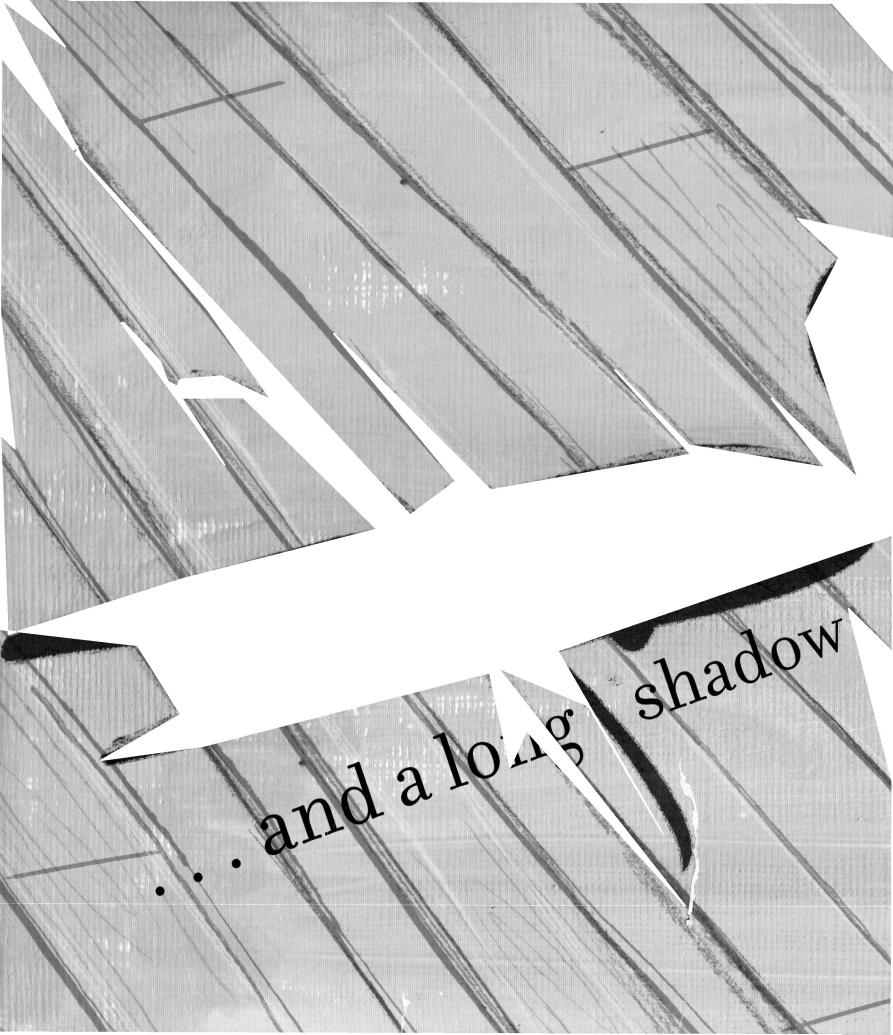

. . . and a long shadow

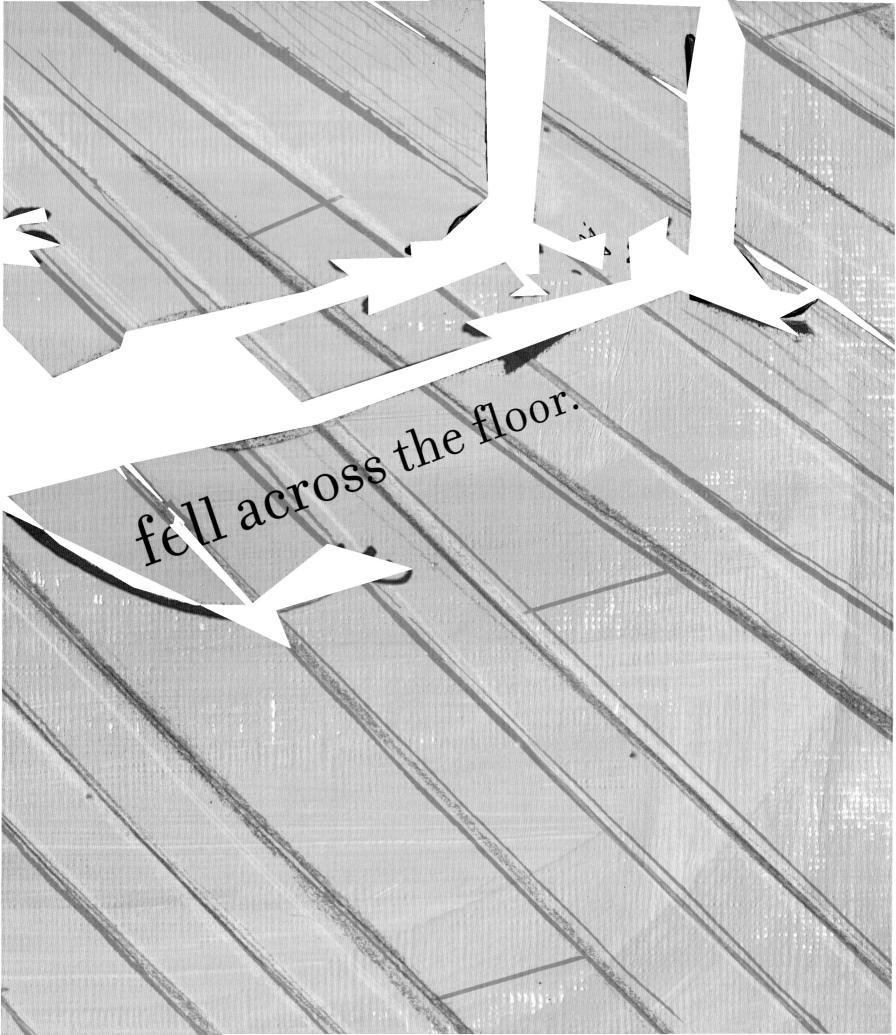

fell across the floor.

"Sizzling sea snakes!" gasped Captain Buckleboots. "It's BIG BAD BILL, the naughtiest cowboy in the Wild, Wild West!"

"And did you know," whispered Captain Buckleboots,
"that apart from all the usual **bad** things, like . . .

CATTLE RUSTLING . . .

ha ha!

HOLD-UPS . . .

and **REFUSING** to take his boots off in the bath . . .

BIG BAD BILL has **never** been known to apologize to anyone for **ANYTHING!**"

"You mean he's NEVER said sorry?"
said Sam. "That can't be true!"

But it was.

"I just never felt the need . . ." shrugged
BIG BAD BILL as he made himself comfortable.

"But," said Sam, "if you **don't** say sorry
you could stay on the naughty step
longer than you think."

"That's right," gasped Captain Buckleboots. "And they may . . .

take away **special treats** . . .

throw you in **jail** . . .

or EVEN make you walk
the **naughty plank!**"

"And, worst of all," gulped Sam,
"**You-Know-Who** might
find out . . ."

"Shivering snowflakes!"
spluttered Captain Buckleboots.
"You wouldn't want that!"

didn't want to be a BIG BAD BILL any more.

Bad Bill's Good Behaviour chart

No Gold Stars

For Bill

"Don't worry," said Sam. "What you need to do is say that you're **sorry** AND **change your ways**, then you won't be so very bad any more."

Just then a voice
from the kitchen
called,

"You can get off
the naughty step now."

So, with a **smile** and a
wave and a *flick* of a **spur**,

off they all went
to try their **best**

to put things right.

And, **staggering stetsons**,
BIG BAD BILL actually
did say sorry . . .

and **did** change his ways.

And when he'd earned a gold star for good behaviour
nobody ever called him **BIG BAD BILL** again.

As for Captain Buckleboots and Sam,
they both showed that they were truly sorry . . .

"I'm sorry, shipmates," said Captain Buckleboots.

"I'm **SO** sorry, Mummy,"
said Sam.

And because Sam's mum could see he **really** meant it . . .

YiPpEty YeE-HaA!

Soon Sam found himself sitting somewhere much, **much** nicer than the naughty step, having a **very** good time indeed.

For Nick from West to East
M.S.

To Mike with love and thanks
T.M.

PUFFIN BOOKS
Published by the Penguin Group: London, New York,
Australia, Canada, India, Ireland, New Zealand and South Africa
Penguin Books Ltd, Registered Offices:
80 Strand, London WC2R 0RL, England
puffinbooks.com
First published 2012
Text copyright © Mark Sperring, 2012
Illustrations copyright © Tom McLaughlin, 2012
Made and printed in China
ISBN: 978–0–141–34286–3
001 – 10 9 8 7 6 5 4 3 2 1